WHISKEY'S SONG

Mitzi Chandler

Health Communications, Inc.
Pompano Beach, FL

Mitzi Chandler
Port Angeles, Washington

Acknowledgments

An earlier version of "Little Sister" appeared under the title
of "Fish Tank" in PUDDING MAGAZINE. (1984)

Names in the book have been changed.

ISBN 0-932194-42-7

Published by Health Communications, Inc.
            1721 Blount Road
            Pompano Beach, Florida 33069

Cover design by Reta Kaufman

Dedication

To my Mother. A women loved by her six children. A woman with the courage to allow me to tell our story.

You sang to me Whiskey's Song,
you sang my life off key . . .

One

THE PROCESSION

At four
I saw my father
dead drunk
for the first time.

I was sitting
on stepping stones
that led
to our back door.
Scrambled
out of the way
of two grim-faced men
carrying him
by his feet and shoulders.

He looked heavy.
He hung like a hammock.

EMBARRASSED TO DEATH

The first time
I saw Momma's
pubic hair
Daddy was dragging her,
feet first,
to the bathtub
to drown her.

I still hear
the thud
of flailing limbs.
Curses, pleas,
my sister's screams.
Running water.

And I still see
Momma
trying to pull
her dress down
to cover herself.

THE BUCKET OF BLOOD TAVERN

World War II
and the troops are in,
soldiers guzzlin' booze
with the navy men.

Backs gettin' slapped
and backs gettin' stabbed,
asses kicked
and asses grabbed.

Two little girls
sittin' at the bar,
eatin' purple eggs
from a pickle jar.

Drinkin' Coca Cola,
munchin' pretzels and chips,
gettin' sick on whiskey
from sneakin' little sips.

Soldiers give you quarters
if you give 'em a hug,
Momma on the dance floor
cuttin' a rug.

Daddy goes over
yanks Momma's wrist,
guy she's dancin' with
makes a tight fist.

Daddy falls down
with a great big thud,
that's how it goes
at the Bucket of Blood.

THANKSGIVING DINNER

Turkey with trimmings,
sweet-potato pudding, biscuits.
The smell of apple pie
and tension
hang
in the air.

We kids, hungry baby birds,
wait for the feast.
Try not to see
the familiar signs.

Momma in a pretty apron,
skittish as a squirrel.
Daddy at the head of the table,
watches . . . waits.
Then as quick as he can say,
"This turkey is too dry"
it happens.

Crash of glass,
the turkey shatters the window.
Mashed potatoes cling to walls.
Table overturned,
our feast scattered.
Momma sits stunned.
A hurled knife
lodged in her lip.

MY FATHER,
THE ENTERTAINER

STEP RIGHT UP BOYS AND GIRLS
See him juggle not two
but THREE oranges.
He'll make an egg disappear
right before your eyes.

> A calliope plays somewhere . . .
> It must have.

AND OVER HERE IS THE STRONG
MAN
Watch him do push-ups
with not two but ONE hand.
TEST YOUR STRENGTH
Arm wrestle with the man of steel.

> He lets you win sometimes.

AND IN THIS TENT
Guess what he's drawing?
A bird, top hat, an ice-cream cone.
YOU WIN! Give that child a dime.

> Far off I hear applause.

DON'T BE A 'FRAIDY CAT
Step into the dark with monster man.
He crawls on all fours. He growls . . .
I GOTCHA!

> Ghoulish laughter echoes
> from a chamber.

SEE HIM DISAPPEAR RIGHT DOWN
THE BOTTLE.

TWO-FACED HANDS

I watched my father's
sober hands
weave morning glories
through a garden trellis,
pat soil around zinnias,
marigolds.

I peer through
aquarium bubbles
as his hands fashion
a home of swaying seaweed,
colored pebbles
for angel fish, guppies
black mollies.

At Christmas
his hands create
a sleepy village
under the tree.
Churches, haystacks,
horses, people.
Houses with lights inside.
His brown eyes soft.

I wished as hard
as a child could wish
that whiskey would not
turn his hands
to talons.

ROULETTE

The revolver
chamber twirled.
Click. Click. Click.

I sat
on the other side
of the closed
kitchen door,
shoulders and knees
drawn to my
hammering chest.

He slurred,
"These bullets
have names on them."
Click. Click. Click.

Was he
holding the gun
to Momma's head?
Would Daddy
really do it?

Maybe not sober,
but whiskey
could pull
that trigger.

THE TOOTH FAIRY

She floats through the door
draped in Cannon white,
runs soft fingers
over my face, whispers,
"Are you asleep?"
"Yeth" giggles through.

"Whooo, I am the Tooth Fairy,
here's a dime for your
front tooth."
I peek.
Dark hair curls
around her face;
she smells of cologne,
not beer.
I am breathless,
butterflies tickle.
"Whooo . . ."
She tiptoes away,
her hands weave the air
with magic.
I want to hug her
forever.

SCAPEGOAT

No one home but me
curled in a chair
watching the new TV.
Hear the doorknob jiggle
like it does
when Daddy's loaded.

"Where's your no-good
Mother?
Who said you could
watch my TV?"

He grabs my braids,
yanks my head back,
pins me in the chair
with his knees.
His face to mine,
mouth and teeth
snap and snarl.
Bites of mad-dog
words spit over me
until I lie limp
in his grip.
Whimpers give way
to sobs.

"Little sissy baby.
Look at the little
sissy baby.
You want a bottle
little sissy baby?"

He yanks the television
and leaves the house,
laughing.

CIGARETTES

Uncle Edgar
smoked in bed.
Uncle Edgar
drunk, then dead.

IN THE HALLWAY

In the hallway
images stare from memory
like wax statues.
I watch a neighbor
in a rage of jealousy
throw his pregnant wife
down the steps.
Then see his fists crack
against Daddy's jaw,
distort his face
like pictures
in boxing magazines.
Hear the squish of saliva.
Watch as blows make
each strand of black hair
stand on end
one by one
as if in slow motion.

In the hallway
I watch
my fourteen-year-old brother,
protecting my mother
fling amateur fists,
afraid to stop until
Daddy lay unconscious;
His eyes blue bulges.
Walls splattered with blood
from father and son.

In this hallway
two teen-age boys,
friends of my sister,
kick my father
in the stomach and head
until he is a bloody, limp rag.
Mother and daughter
begging them to stop.

Even now,
the antics of
Popeye and Bluto,
Tom and Jerry
make me uneasy.
Take me back
to the hallway.

CHRISTMAS EVE

It took him
hours to decorate
the ceiling-high tree.
Arrange the lights
in a pattern of
red, blue, yellow.
Christmas balls
spaced just so.
A star on top.
We kids drape tinsel
on the lower branches,
one strand at a time.
The final magic,
he dresses his creation
in a gossamer gown
of angel hair.

Under the tree
he fashions
a snow-covered farm.
Haystacks snipped
from broom straws,
fence posts handcut
from twigs.
He lets us place
a sheep here, a horse there,
rearranges what we did.
I pretend happy people live
in the farm house

with a light.
Happy, like I feel.

It took him seconds
to topple the tree.
The snow-covered farm
scattered in a rumple
of white sheet.
Tree lights blinking
merrily,
as if they didn't know.

DIRTY WORK

I   That's what you do
when you're a kid
livin' with drunk grown-ups.
Pourin' pee outta shoes,
wipin' up blood,
cleanin' up vomit.

II   Holes all over the house.
Black snake come up through one.
Daddy chopped off its head,
tells me, "Clean it up."
Poor two-piece wigglin' snake.

III   Aquarium shattered
by flyin' chairs.
Little fish on the floor
gettin' squashed.
Makes my sister and me cry
when we pick 'em up.
'Specially Black Molly.

IV   Momma says, "Sneak in
and get some money outta
Daddy's pants."
He's sleepin' off a drunk.
I'm scared to death
he's gonna wake up
and catch me.
Money jingles loud
when you're sneakin'.

V   Strange man in bed
with Momma.
Pretend I don't see
when I go by the door.
She says, "Get me a cigarette."
She don't even care
that I saw.

VI   Daddy comes home drunk,
says, "Where's your
Goddamn mother?"
I mumble, "I don't know"
like she told me.
Know I'm gonna get the belt.
Just glad to get it over.

VII   Little brother and sisters
scared and cryin'.
Daddy got 'em on his lap
tellin' how Poppa Bear
is a good guy
and Momma Bear is a slut.
I pull the kids away,
try to hold him down.
Don't even feel
when my lip puffs up.

Then I wipe up the blood.
That's dirty work.

MY SISTER'S PARTY

Be a good girl
and Daddy will give
you a party.

She opens
the front door,
giggly friends
by her side, expecting
balloons, ice cream,
her cake with nine candles.
Finds Daddy
sprawled on the floor.
Naked.

Four wide-eyed girls
stare at his limp penis.
Her face burns
as she backs out the door,
mumbles an apology
to her friends
who run down the steps
in clumsy silence.

At thirteen, my sister
painted her lips
angry red,
got knocked up,
went to reform school.

VISITING RELATIVES

At Aunt Ida's
the grown-ups guzzle booze,
play poker, eat salt herring.
Us kids drink cokes,
eat donuts, candy.
Eddie sneaks sips of whiskey.

Sissy rides a bike
in the living room,
dodging dog doo.
Tommy farts every five seconds.
Eddie tells Aunt Ida he's
going to be sick.
She cups her hands,
catches every drop.
Goes back to poker.

Kids wind down like toys,
nod off on chairs.
Grown-ups stagger upstairs
to bed. Uncle Ed
sleeps at the table,
false teeth in his hand.

Faucet drips, mosquito buzzes,
grown-ups snore.
Tommy farts in his sleep.
I flick on the kitchen light,
watch roaches scurry off
the left-over deli food.

Momma says Aunt Ida
doesn't cook, sends out.
Doesn't wash clothes,
buys new.
Uncle Ed's a plumber,
makes good money.
They drink a lot,
but don't fight
like at our house.
Aunt Ida's funny
but she laughs too hard,
hurts feelings,
plays pranks on her kids.
Little Eddie's got sad eyes.
Uncle Ed is quiet.

I go upstairs,
watch people sleep,
look in closets,
stare at the clock.
At the table, Uncle Ed grunts.
I cover his teeth
with a napkin,
count chips, make card houses.
Watch a fly stuck
on the sticky paper overhead.

WATCHING

Poker chips clink.
Smoke hovers.
Whiskey, straight.

Eyes at half-mast,
he brags to my father,
"Had her spayed,
she's always sprawled
and ready."
Runs hairy hands
up bare legs, open legs.

She smells of woman,
her skin dull as
dirty laundry.
Brushes her square teeth
with salt and finger.
Tells of knitting needle
abortions.

Later, the man snores
at the table.
She and Daddy are gone.
My mother cries.

I watch.
Wish away the bumps
forming on my chest.

LOCKED IN

We heard the nails
being hammered
in the door.
His assurance
we couldn't return
while he slept off
a drunk.

A round-bellied mother,
three children
locked out
on a January night.

"Why don't you
leave him, Momma?"

"Because," she says.
Her voice
on the edge.

IT WASN'T SUPPOSED TO BE LIKE THIS

Go to our house to clean
before Momma comes home
from the hospital
with my sister.
Daddy drops me off,
goes to Neddie's Bar.

Daddy's back. I'm a mess
from scrubbing floors.
He said he'd take me back
to Aunt Ida's before
we go see Momma.
Going to curl my hair,
wear my pink dress.
I'll pass for fourteen.

Open the car door to get in,
dog beats me to it.
Daddy cusses at me,
say's it's my fault
Spot won't budge.
Daddy comes 'round my side,
slaps my face a few times,
pulls the dog out,
shoves me in.

We don't go to Aunt Ida's,
instead go to Neddie's Bar.
He buys me a coke, pours salt
in his beer. Says, "You look
cheap in a sweater. You're
no good just like your mother."
Pokes his finger against my chest.

Men are looking.
I ask to go to the restroom,
sneak out the backdoor.
The car's locked so I cry
on the hood in broad daylight.
A long time later he comes out,
slaps me around for walking
out on him.

We weave in heavy traffic.
He gets out to pee
at a stop light.
I scoot down in the seat.
He says how grateful
I should be he buys groceries.
How he had to get married,
things like that.
I say, "Let's not go see Momma."

In the hospital I walk
behind him. People stare.
My hair's messy,
eyes all puffy. A nun looks
like she's going to say something,
but she doesn't.

Momma's alone in a big ward.
She looks so pretty
sitting up in bed, a pink ribbon
in her pageboy.
Her eyes tear when she sees us.
It wasn't supposed to be like this.
I wanted to make her happy,
bring flowers, wear my pink dress.

She says, "What have you done
to the child?"
He calls us both sluts, staggers
out, tells me to find my own way home.

I hug Momma, cry. Ask about
my new sister.
She is in an incubator.
So small.
I feel sad she has to live
at our house.
I tell Momma not to worry,
I'll find my way home.
Walk, ride the bus, but don't worry.

I don't have any money, don't know
who to call.
Daddy's outside. Follows me
up the street in the car,
calling me names.
Traffic slows, horns honk.
I walk fast, look the other way.
"Get in," he orders.
At first I don't. Then I do.
Don't know my way home.

Two

ROLE REVERSAL

Big Brother's
been kicked out.
I'm thirteen; oldest
home now.

Tonight they're at it
again.
Kids clingin' to me.
Something snaps.
I can't take it no more.
I shove Daddy
down in a chair.
Scream, "We can't go on
livin' like this!"
Momma laughs, kind of nervous
'cause I pushed him.
I scold, "You shouldn't be
drinkin', baby's due anyday."
Yellin', my arms swingin',
I feel like an ape showin'
how fierce I am. Bluffin'.
I knock over a lamp, get scared
run out the door and hide in a barn
under dryin' tobacco leaves.
Heart poundin', sobbin'.
Somethin' changes inside.

Next mornin' they're fightin'
before the rooster crows.
Momma in bed,
sprained her ankle
last night.
He starts over to hit her.
I jump up on the bed
make a real fist,
say, "Don't you dare
hit my Momma."
Daddy glares up at me,
my hackles raised,
and backs off.

I feel like a grizzly
protectin' her cub.
The roles are set.
I'm not helpless anymore.

LITTLE SISTER

Daddy liked to
hold her
upside down
in the aquarium
until she stopped
squirming.
Terrified eyes
look out.
Curious fish nibble
at her cheeks.

In the womb
she had beans
and fatback,
but mostly booze.

I was fourteen,
helped the whiskey-weaving
driver steer the car,
held the broken door shut.
Momma in the back
in the grip of labor
and a vomit hangover.

Four-pound survivor
born hungover.
Large eyes,
face flat,
pressed against a wall
of a fish tank.

DAY AFTER PAYDAY

Hadn't been for Momma
or maybe because
of Momma
my life might of ended
at age fourteen.
Head split
right down the middle.

Was early mornin'.
Kitchen table
turned on its side,
toast squashed,
milk spilled.
Daddy slappin' Momma,
kids squattin' in the corner,
cryin'.
Better try 'n' stop it
before it gets too bad.

I get between 'em.
Daddy's eyes
just this side of crazy.
He ain't drunk yet
and he's strong.
Momma gets
the coal stove poker,
starts comin' at him.

He grabs it, shoves her
out the screen door
and heads toward me.
That poker over his head
in both hands,
murder on his face.
I put my arms
over my head,
close my eyes tight.
Don't know what
I'm thinkin'
but before he comes down
on my head with that thing
Momma grabs it,
runs out the back door.
So does he.

I hush the kids,
pick up the table,
scrub the floor,
go to school.

INFIRMARY

Even a savior cries
when hell
is hotter than usual.
Quiver-chinned girl
seeks comfort
from the school nurse.
She glances at the girl,
directs her to the bed,
says "Don't get lipstick
on my pillow case."

WHISKEY'S SONG

Once I heard
my Father whistle
and my breath caught
in my throat.

"Oh Daddy, don't.
I only know
your whiskey song.
Don't stir my longing
for a melody
that cannot be.
Your moment of peace
will vanish
and I'll know
our loss more
for having heard
the song
that could have been."

VOYEURS

In the tenement hall
neighbor men gather,
leer through the open door
as father and teen-aged daughter
draw blood.

Ringside,
they stare
as fists pound.
Stare
as seams rip
from a summer blouse.
Stare
as he falls,
the back of his neck
punctured
by sharp metal that juts
from a radiator.

Round one hundred.
This time she wins.
She closes the door
on voyeur eyes,
picks up the limp loser,
fixes his wounds.

NURSERY RHYME

He huffs and puffs
and blows the house down.
Three little faces
hide behind a couch.
Between muffled sobs
fear sings a nursery rhyme.

"He's our Papa
but he ain't no good.
Let's chop him up
for kindlin' wood."

ESCAPE

The six-year-old girl
creeps around
her father
passed out on the floor.
She unlatches the front door,
returns upstairs
to get her brother and sister.
Tiny sobs escape
as three children
ease out the door to safety
at a neighbor's house.
Momma goes there
when she's kicked out.

When he wakes
they see him
behind the screendoor,
glaring.
He motions them to return.
Tiny sobs escape
as they scurry home.
Too afraid and small
to do anything else.

BREAKING

Hammer in hand
I smash again and again
a case of beer
sitting on the table.
White foam spurts
over my father's face,
my mother's dress.
Droopy eyes now wide,
mouths gape, silent.
Knowing it could be them.

OUT OF REACH

What hurts
is that
love
cries out
on the other side
of a wall
we don't know
how
to climb.

A WAY OF RELATING

You really do see stars
when you're hit hard enough.
Waiting for my boyfriend —
primping — when all hell
breaks loose in the kitchen.
I run downstairs,
pull Daddy off Momma.
He turns, his fist
cracks hollow on my jaw.
I hit the stove, slide to the floor.
There they are — those stars —
right overhead.
When the room comes back,
Daddy is smacking Momma's face,
her head going this way then that.
I grab him tight around the neck,
too afraid to let go.
Look up in time to see
Momma come down on his head,
hard as she can with that
coal stove poker.
I raise my hand to stop the blow.
It busts my thumb, splits his head.
Blood gushes over my green jumper.
He falls to the floor.
I know he saw stars.

We shake him awake. Put ice on his head.
Fix Momma's lip, my thumb.
Kids come out from behind the couch.
We cry, hug each other,
say how sorry we are.
Grab love where we find it.

CONTACT

Sometimes,
fighting
is better
than walking
on eggs.
Anger
can embrace
when arms
aren't able.
Easier
to live
in chaos
than a void.

INSTRUCTIONS
FROM BIG SISTER

When a fight is brewing
get under the bed,
cover your ears
with your pillow
and everything will be okay.

They believed me.
They believed in me.

I had to be brave.

MOVING DAYS

I   Acme Storage man apologized
when he took the crib,
again when he took
the high chair.
Asked Momma how a man could
do this to his family.
Left some blankets.

Empty rooms echo.
Candles flicker shadows,
nursery rhymes soothe.
Worry about tomorrow,
tomorrow.

II   Yesterday I lived
on Barnaby Road.
Stayed the night
with a friend,
dropped off at home.
Everything's gone.
No note.
Neighbor said
he moved them out this morning,
"I think your Ma said Hillside."
Packed my hurt,
hunted for home.

III   A Melodrama:
        "You must pay the rent."
        "I can't pay the rent."
        (Hero not around.)

        Sofa, stove, beds, toys,
        sit under a street light.
        Snow falls on a sidewalk auction.
        Going, going . . . gone.

IV   Spatulas with sheets,
        aspirin with shoes.
        Little faces
        among packed belongings.
        Mother passed-out
        on mattress ticking,
        birth control jelly
        on bedroom floor.
        Uncle has been to help.

        Grown sister comes home.
        I make a game of setting up house.
        Spatula in drawer,
        sheets in cupboard,
        aspirin in cabinet,
        shoes in closet.
        Coffee for Mother.
        Hide the greasy tube.

        Three kids play.
        Crayons, comics,
        pick-up-sticks.

DILEMMA

I ought to call
the police.
Dirty Lady said I could
use her phone.
She's stirrin' sauerkraut
seasoned with slimy pig tails.
I sit by the phone
in a dumpyard chair
hoppin' with fleas
and think:

Momma where are you?
You've been gone
five days now.
You left with Dirty Lady's brother;
He said he left you
in Freddie's Bar
but I don't believe him.
He's got mean eyes.
I looked everywhere,
even went to the old neighborhoods
to see if you were with those drinkin'
friends.

We're outta food
and I'm missin' a lot of school
watchin' the kids.
I know I should call the police
but if I do and you're
just out drunk,
they'll take the little ones away.

God! I can't do that.
But what if you are hurt
or dead?
Why are you doing this
to me?

I find her the next day,
vomit on her dress,
hair a rat's nest.
Pretty face all puffy.
She cries.
I hold her.
Nobody can hurt you
like a Momma.

CHRISTMAS BASKET

Seven cans of pumpkin,
a chewed rubber toy.
Puzzle, missing pieces,
soiled shirt for a boy.
Ham and sweet potatoes,
assorted broken games.
Cans with no labels,
for people with no names.

TRANSFER

My high school friends
and I squeeze onto
the crowded city bus.
I see my father slouched
behind the driver —
the seat facing the aisle —
head nodding, fly open.
The hiss of the closing door
wakes him.
His eyes focus on me.

"Hey, come sit on your
Daddy's lap, honey."

Over the hush
I whisper,
"May I have a transfer?"

"Goddamn you're pretty,
come sit on my lap."

The knot of strangers stare
as I push to the back of the bus,
teeth and transfer clenched.
Wait
for the next stop.

LAVENDER'S BLUE

I scream an endless scream
from a rooftop.
Dream of mutilated bodies
that wake me in a clammy sweat.

* * * * * *

I wore a sweater, ran home
when a man whistled.
Cried in the closet.
Pulled down windowshades
of purple;
Momma's favorite color.
I loved her quilt.
Now I hate lavender.
Men touch lavender.
Lavender's blue.

* * * * * *

Salt brine in the pantry
next to trash cans of beer,
next to the coal stove.
All the drunk soldiers.
Momma gave me five dollars
to leave so her man wouldn't look
at me.
I knocked him over
when he pulled me on his lap.

He made minute steaks
for my mother.
Minute men.
<u>Sixty Minute Man</u>
They called him lovin' Dan . . .
Didn't know what that meant.

* * * * * *

Two bits, four bits.
Drunk soldiers
gave a little girl
silver dollars
if she could stand them on end.
Also gave her money
not to tell her Momma
what they tried to do.
Bucky, with thick inside-out lips
(or was that Uncle Edgar?)
picks her up between her legs
to show her the horses.
Picks her up between her legs
and she wants DOWN.

I WANT DOWN!

I WANT OUT!

I want to choke somebody.

FATHER-DAUGHTER TALK

Once
in a moment
of sober sanity
you said
casually,
"Tell me your problems."

The lump
that lived
in my throat
grew larger.
I wanted to
pour out the ocean,
but I had lived
too long
on shifting sands.

That you asked
was enough.

CAUGHT IN A BOTTLE

My mother sways
behind the screendoor.
She has so many fears,
one of them is wind.

I lean defying
the wind.
Trash cans tumble by.
Trees bend in submission
or snap
as backs are broken.
A storm whirls around me,
in me.

Her words wail.
"Come inside.
God will punish you."

Inside, a family swirls,
caught in a bottle.
They twist and turn
until mother is child,
child is parent,
father is enemy.

In its calm,
sullen quiet
measures every breath.
We watch over shoulders
wary of the sudden howl
of whisky wind.

Windows are closed.
Pressure builds.
Shatters.

Outside, under God's sky,
I pit myself
against the storm.
Pray the wind
will carry me away
to Kansas,
or anywhere.

HOMECOMING

Summer away,
a carefree time.
Dread returns
as I turn onto our street.
The house is dark.
The smell of cigarettes,
stale beer hangs
in humid night air.
I trip as I cross
to turn on the light.
A dull overhead bulb
brought me home.

Lamps, couch, chairs,
toppled over.
Plastic curtains
pulled from rods.
Daddy's clothes scattered.
He is sprawled
on the linoleum.
My little brother
curled beside him.
I take the sleeping
boy upstairs,
rock him to soothe
my ache.

Momma and the girls
at a neighbor's.
Her face weighed down
from beer and beatings.

Said she didn't want me
to come home to this.
Kids wanted to make
a welcome sign.
Have balloons.

Pigtailed waifs
in dresses too big,
faces too wise.
Somersaults, piggyback,
story telling.
Then sleep
in big sister's arms.

LEAVING

I'm leaving home
but how can I?

The little ones
will surely cry.

I need them
and they need me.

I'm leaving home
but I won't be free.

HOPE CHEST

You
in a haze,
half-aware
of my graduation.

I
in a dream
that you will give me
a hope chest;
A tradition for a girl
on this day.

This chest would hold
a music box that plays
You're Daddy's Little Girl.

A note on blue paper
that says, "Forgive me."

A valentine heart
on white lace.

A velvet pillow.

At seventeen,
I know that dreams,
some dreams,
can't come true.

But I hope for
a token of your love.
I need a place
to fold away the pain.

THE LAST STOP

He drove a city bus,
night shift.
Brought home transfers
for the kids to play with.
Got fired — drunk on the job.

Made a little money
working for his brother —
when he was sober.
Rode the bus between
Denny's Bar and a dingy room.

After that,
spent his days on the bench
at 5th and Mellon —
the last stop.

BUM AT THE BUS STOP

Rumpled clothes,
shaggy hair.
That's my father,
lying there.

Three

WEDDING GIFT

We found my father
on his bench,
told him of our wedding.
Uncle Paul would give me away.
He was glad of that.
Said he didn't think
he could come.

* * * * * *

With the first strains
of the Wedding March
I heard the church door creak.
My father stepped in,
a rumpled hat
atop a gaunt face.
He nodded a sober head,
looked into my eyes.

I walked down the aisle
seeing not my groom
but that broken man.
When the vows were over,
I looked back.
He was gone.
But he had come.

BEFORE THEY CALLED
IT A DISEASE

He once said,
"When you grow up,
you'll see it wasn't
all my fault . . ."

He meant my mother.

Now I know it wasn't
all his fault . . .
or my mother's.

They both died
again and again,
not knowing
who's fault it was.

GALLERY

There is a gallery
on a street where I often go.
Just inside
hangs a black and white
photograph of a woman.
Half her face in soft light,
an aura highlights dark hair.
On the other half, light comes
from below, casting harsh shadows.
Her eyes, hollow sockets.
It is titled <u>Saint and Sinner</u>.
This picture is too easy.

As I wander I see a painting
of the same woman,
her hair a bounce of curl.
She smiles, folds towels
with a small girl.
A boy plays with a kitten.
The colors are clear, defined.

In another painting
the woman wears a lavender sweater,
a quiver of mouth.
She sits by a window as if waiting;
As if she has waited forever.

In one, a man holds his fist
in her face.
In another, shoves her from behind.
Her dress stretched over a belly,
full with baby.
Her eyes, empty.

On a gray wall
portraits hang off-center.
Older now,
the woman sits at a bar,
a stranger's hand around her waist.
A girl tugs at her arm.
The woman pushes her away.
And then,
watercolors.
Muddy fingers of color
bleed into one another,
distort her face . . .

Black and white
is too easy.

TOO LITTLE

You planted
zinnias, morning glories,
marigolds, roses.

You painted
men in fedoras,
faces in half-shadow.

You clapped
when I memorized
Dick and Jane.

You gave
a girl in braids
a small glass dog.

You kept
an aquarium.
We gave names to the fish.

You fixed
a dinner with
three kinds of potatoes.

You created
a sleepy village
under the Christmas tree.

You said
read the encyclopedia,
seek peace of mind.

You bragged
I was a lefty like you,
threw a ball like a boy.

You made
Plaster of Paris ducks,
horses, the crucifix.

You destroyed
yourself with whiskey
before I had enough of you.

BLACKOUTS

I live in your blackouts,
remember what you can't recall
when whiskey floods,
spills in a torrent
of hissing words.
Crumples a child's heart.

I remember when madness
from a bottle
tightens hands into fists.
Loosens hands that invade
the unfolding
from child to woman.

What you can't recall
is mine
to mend for a lifetime.

BEFORE HEALING

Get off the stage!
The play is over.
The actors gone,
taken new roles.
Some have died.

I can't.
I was born
in the play.
Scenes whirled
around me;
I had no lines.

I can't shed
my costume.
The skin
I live in.

PENT UP

Inside me
was a grotesque
three-headed
jack-in-the-box.

Ugly bobbing heads
lurched out
of a dark place
to taunt me.

Their raucous voices
vibrated through my veins.
Only a blood-letting
quieted them.

METAMORPHOSIS

Somewhere in the haze
of my childhood
Snow White and Wonderwoman
became my heroines.
Virtue. Strength.
Absolutes needed
to keep afloat
in the bubbling brew.

In my yearbook a friend wrote . . .

Ninety-nine and forty-four
One hundred percent pure.

Another . . .

To the bravest girl
I ever knew.

Long after childhood,
make-believe ended.
Snow White and Wonderwoman
were swallowed
in the fiery breath
of a dragon.
And slowly,
out of their ashes,
I began to emerge.
Tarnished, frightened,
but at long last,
real.

WHITEWASH

White was the color
of lies
told to protect,
to hide the shame.

The Holy in white
called it sin.
Healers in white
prescribed pills,
will power.

White is the color
of the teeth
of policemen who smile,
pat the back
of the wife abuser.

Even in death
white shrouds the face
of alcoholism.

MEDICAL REPORT

August 24, 1977

This 65-year-old male
had a left upper neck dissection
and excision of a lesion
of the left hard palate.

Squamous Carcinoma

Patient was recently seen
with an extensive tumor involving
the hard and soft palate and extending
bilaterally in the tonsillar fossa
and left retro-molar area.

Epidermoid Carcinoma

This disease is very advanced
and unrespectable.
Prognosis is very poor.
The patient should be considered
for complete disability.

Respectfully,

Ralph McCormick, MD
Chief, Department of Radiation Therapy

* * * * * * *

April 10, 1980
Precipitating   cause: Alcohol   and
cigarettes.
Regretfully,
His daughter

MY FATHER'S ROOM

The attic room is hot,
reeks from months of garbage.
Roaches crawl over
rotting hamburgers,
cans of soup,
cartons of eggnog.
Maggots wriggle in plastic cups
of congealed urine.
Napkins scrumpled with cancerous spit.
This debris piled along one wall,
almost orderly.

My sister and I don't look at each other.
We are trash collectors
cleaning bits and pieces
of what remains of our father.
We sweep, spray, scrub.
Change yellowed sheets.
Bag garbage and empty bottles
of Thunderbird stowed under the bed.

He sits in a chair wiping his mouth.
Watching.
Ninety pounds. Mouth and throat
eaten by cancer.
Whiskey brain.
He's not violent now.
We say it's hot. He nods.
He says it's hot. We agree.
What do you say to your father's bones?

Strewn about on a bedstand,
on a table, in drawers
are notes written to his brother.
Shopping lists.

BOLT   HASP   LOCK

written on scraps of paper,
matchbook covers, napkins, cardboard.

BOLT   HASP   LOCK   GLUE

pictures drawn of them.
You can still see his talent for drawing.

Scattered around and in scrapbooks
are pictures cut from magazines.
Bobcat, bear, pheasant, bowls of fruit,
sunsets, salmon jumping, cocktails.
We sort through the musty paper,
sneak some for ourselves.

We tell him we are sorry there had been
no help.
Half of his mouth says,
"It's a terrible thing."

That night my sister and I
divide our paper treasures,
put them in baggies.
It's all we have of him.

BOLT   HASP   LOCK

His life scribbled on paper.

THE CALL

She phoned to tell me
Daddy had died.

"Thanks for calling,"
I said, and returned
to dusting.

Three days later
I called Father Joe,
a recovering alcoholic.
A slight burning in my nose
as I said,
"My Father finally died."

I had grieved
his life,
there was none left
for his death.

WHISKEY TALK

My Father
didn't know how to say,
I'm lost, I hurt, help me.
He roared drunken profanities.
King of his jungle.
Twenty years we shuddered
at his roar.

Whiskey stole his thunder.
Cancer ate his mouth.
From the hospital bed
he rasped,
"YouNoGoodGodDamnSonofaBitch
Fuckin' Bastard"
to my Mother
who had phoned in sympathy.
They had not spoken
in fifteen years.
There were tears in his eyes.
I saw them.

Cancer consumed his throat.
He couldn't speak.
From a nursing home bed he scrawled,
"Get me some Muscatel."
My sister shook her head no.
His eyes glared
YouNoGoodGodDamnSonofaBitch
Fuckin' Bastard.

No resting place.
His ashes scratched onto
his Mother's grave.
My sister knelt,
tears made mud
of the soil she caressed.
I stood above her,
whispered an epitaph.
YouNoGoodGodDamnSonofaBitch
Fuckin' Bastard,
I loved you.